MARIA ZACHARIA

Little Johnny's Dreamland

Illustration: Evi Tsaknia

Traslated from Greek: Karen Emmerich

Additional copies of Little Johnny's Dreamland may be purchased using the order forms in the back of the book or by writing to:

Little Johnny's Dreamland
P.O. Box 3341
Memphis, TN 38173-0341

Copyright© Maria Zacharia
Copyright for the Illustration© Evi Tsaknia
Translated from Greek: Karen Emmerich
Art directions: Peritechnon, 10th Nikaias str. 104 34 Athens, Hellas

ISBN 978-0-9800823-0-2

Manufactured in the United States of America.

First Printing 2007   6,000 copies

MERCURY
PRINT · DIGITAL · FULFILLMENT
A CONSOLIDATED GRAPHICS COMPANY

People, even little children, often find themselves in serious and difficult
situations, facing problems that demand great courage and daring to overcome.
One day, little Johnny found himself faced with just such a problem, something that made
him very sad and worried. How would he overcome it? What should he do?

That night when he went to bed he wasn't laughing and joking as he usually was,
but sad and thoughtful, his little eyes brimming with tears. But when he
finally fell asleep, he suddenly found himself standing in a bright green field in front of a
gate covered with flowers! He took a few hesitant steps, then passed through the gate,
and into a wonderful world full of adventures, stories, and dreams!

That's how Johnny's trip to Dreamland began, His journey taught him alot
about love and friendship. Most of all, it taught him that when you have
faith and make use of your strengths you can get through
anything – anything at all, even the hardest, most difficult times!

Our Story

Yanni was a very healthy, happy, handsome little boy. We were a pretty normal family, going about our everyday life. One day, a day like any other, Yanni woke up and started complaining about being tired. A few days later he started complaining about feeling pain in almost every bone in his body. A short while later, we were told that he has ALL (acute lymphoblastic leukemia), Cancer of the blood.

That was the day that our life turned upside-down, our hearts stopped, and our minds started floating between ignorance, despair, and determination to find a cure.

The good news, because you're always looking for good news even in the hardest times, was that Yanni was a low-risk patient. But the bad news came even faster; there was a complication in his case. Yanni started to have multiple headache attacks so severe that all he could do was hold his head in his hands and scream his heart out. An MRI found a huge amount of blood around his brain and his spinal cord. Nobody knew what to do. All they knew was what not to do, he was not allowed to move, at all. Any movement he made could paralyze him from his waist down or cause unknown damage to his brain. We started looking all over the world for a solution. Fast, because time was not on our side.

One day, we received an e-mail from St. Jude Children's Research Hospital. The doctors at the Leukemia clinic and the hospital's research team where interested in Yanni's case. His condition had previously only been a hypothetical complication; now it was captured on an MRI.

I remember the doctors telling us, "We think you should come here as soon as possible. We think we can help Yanni." Those were the magic words that gave us our hope back and Yanni his second chance for life.

Now, my son is almost through the woods. We are finishing our chemo in late September 2007. As I am writing this, he is running around me screaming, jumping, and making funny faces at me. He was four when we came here. Now he is seven. He is very tall for his age. I think he is still very handsome, and for sure he is very happy.

That is my Yanni's story.

With love from Yanni's mom to him …
*   and to all the children of the world.*

This book is dedicated to my son,
Yanni, my daughter, Mariella, to my
husband, Pano, and all the children of St. Jude,
as well as to Dr. Pui and Dr. Mirro,
who gave Yanni a second chance for life.

And ... to my parents for always believing in me.

Special Thanks to those who
supported this printing:

Mr. Tom and Susan Sinis
Mr. Harry and Magda Sinis
Mr. Bill Sinis
Mr. Sarantos and
    Cathy Hatzigeorgiou
Mr. Chris Hatzigeorgiou
Mr. Nick Adamopoulos
Mr. Pete Maragos
Mr. Charles E. Dickey, Jr.
    and Judith M. Dickey
First State Bank
Mr. David Murray
Mr. Bill and Georgia Douklias
Mr. Nicholas Economides
Mr. Bill Mc.Goan
Mr. Jim Rouvelas

First South Bank
Bank of Ripley
Mr. Lee Theodore
Mr. Jim Adamopoulos
Mr. Gabriel G. Couloubaritsis
Mr. Jerry G. Couloubaritsis
Mr. Judd S. Tashie
Mr. and Mrs. Mauraganis
Mr. Paul Tashie
Mr. Charles Vergos
Mr. James Skefos
Wolf River Motors, LLC
Jim's Place East, Inc.
Mr. Tommy and Rebekah Bruce
Gulliver's Travel Co.

Little Johnny's Dreamland

It was a beautiful day and Johnny and his mother decided to go on an outing together. It was Saturday, so Johnny, who was five years old and in kindergarten, didn't have school. One idea was for them to go to the amusement park, since the wind had died down and the sun was shining in the sky. Winter was nearing its end and the day was one of the nicest of the whole season, almost as fine as the halcyon days at the end of autumn. Since the weather was so wonderful, they dressed up in warm clothes and headed for the amusement park.

When they got there, they saw that it was very crowded, lots of kids seemed to have had the same idea. Johnny and his mother parked, got out of the car, and walked hand in hand toward the entrance. Once they were inside, the hours passed in a flash. Whenever you're at the amusement park you always forget to look at your watch and when they finally looked, they saw that it was time for lunch. "We'd better hurry home," said Johnny's mother, "everyone will be waiting for us!" And indeed, they had left everyone back at home: Johnny's father, his sister, and his grandmother, who was visiting the family that day. Johnny's sister, Maria, hadn't come with them because she was in second grade and had homework to do. She preferred to miss the morning outing so that she could go to a friend's house that afternoon, as she had arranged the previous day.

Johnny and his mother had been having such a wonderful time that he wanted to stay even longer. His mom was in a good mood, so she promised him that they could go again that

afternoon. Where to? They'd decide when the time came.

By the time they got home it was two-thirty, everyone was starving, and the table was set. They quickly washed their hands, and then the whole family sat down to eat lunch together that lovely Saturday afternoon.

"Boy, Maria, you sure missed out!" Johnny said, his mouth full of spaghetti and meat sauce. "We went up on the big Ferris wheel and the sky was so clear we could see all the way to the island way off in the distance. The sea was full of big ships and little boats. The sun was so bright that the whole sea was glittering and it hurt my eyes to look at it, but it was so pretty that I kept on looking anyhow."

"Don't talk with your mouth full," his mom said. "You'll choke and besides, it isn't good manners."

"Okay, okay," Johnny said, turning his attention to his food. He certainly had lots more he wanted to tell Maria about, but he was also very hungry. So, Johnny fell silent and sank into his own thoughts. "How nice it would be if there were a place just for kids where only magical

8

things happened ..." Johnny couldn't finish his thought because he suddenly realized that his mother was talking to him.

"Johnny, Johnny, are you all right? Why are you so flushed?"

It was true, he was a little flushed, and felt like he'd eaten way too much. "Come here so I can take your temperature. You seem a little feverish to me," his mom continued, putting her hand on his forehead.

The "procedure," as his mother called it, was simple. "We just stick the thermometer in your mouth, keep it there for a minute, take it out and look." This time it showed 101.5. Sure enough, he had a fever. And of course everyone said that the sun was all fine and good, and the amusement park too, but look what happens if you're not careful and overexert yourself. Well, Johnny thought, I don't see what being careful has to do with it, but then his legs started hurting, they must be a little tired from all the jumping up and down he'd done on the trampoline. So his mother took him to his room, helped him undress and lie down, gave him a pill, and in all the fuss and commotion going on around him somehow he fell asleep.

The next day the whole family went to the doctor's office. They did different tests on him and when they were done everyone sat down to wait for the results. Johnny's mom and dad were a little worried, as for Johnny, despite his fever, he just kept wondering when he could go back to school and see his friend John (all in all there were three Johns at his school) and play ball with him during recess.

At some point the doctor came out and called Johnny's parents into his office. He didn't know how much time passed, but when they came out they were very upset, and from then on everything happened very quickly. They didn't go back home again, his parents took Johnny straight to the hospital because the doctor said he was very sick and they had to give him some medicine right away so that he could get better. Johnny had no idea how he ended up in the hospital room. His mom was with him the whole time, though his dad had gone home to get Johnny's pajamas and some other things.

The doctors came and went and gave Johnny lots of disgusting medicine, put needles in his arm that hurt a lot, and even then he still had a fever and was so tired from his very long and difficult day that as soon as he closed his eyes he fell right asleep.

"Or maybe I'm not asleep yet," Johnny thought. He was standing in the middle of a bright green field. In front of him, in the distance, was a huge wall with a gate in the middle that was just slightly ajar. "No, I'm asleep and dreaming," Johnny decided.

The wall with the gate in it looked very beautiful from afar, but no matter how hard he tried to see what it was made of, he just couldn't tell. So Johnny decided to go closer. As he approached, he was very surprised to see that the wall and the gate were decorated all over with... daisies of all different colors! White ones, pink ones, purple ones, red and blue and yellow and orange.The wall was completely covered with daisies of every conceivable color, and even some colors you couldn't imagine if you tried. Above the gate was an inscription, "DREAMLAND," in big red letters that seemed to glow against the white background of the sign. Johnny's mouth was hanging open in surprise: the colors looked so beautiful together he could hardly believe his eyes.

Suddenly, the gate opened a little bit wider and a creature appeared in front of it, a kind of creature Johnny had never seen before, not even in a book. It was cabbage-colored, with a very small body, small arms and legs, a tiny little head and very long ears. Its body was covered in short fur all over and even from a distance you could tell that it must be very soft.

"Hello, Johnny," the creature said, smiling a huge smile.

The first thought that passed through Johnny's mind was, "How does he know my name?" But since he was always a very polite little boy and also very curious, he answered almost immediately, "Hello! Who are you, and what is this place?"

Johnny must have seemed very confused, because the soft, green little creature immediately came up to him and grabbed his hand, laughing, and pulled him gently toward the half-open gate. "Come on, don't be scared," he said, "I'm Chubby and this is Dreamland. In Dreamland, we all live together, all the characters from comics and fairytales from all over the world, some famous and some not. Only children can visit us, and only in their dreams. Only good, magical things happen here. I'm sure you'll like it very much, and you'll make lots of friends and learn lots of useful things that can help you deal with the difficult situation you're now facing."

"How do you know all that about me?" Johnny asked his new friend, surprised.

"Here in Dreamland, we know everything about the children who come to visit us," Chubby answered. By now, they had passed through the gate and suddenly found themselves in Dreamland.

What can I say?! Johnny couldn't believe his eyes or ears. Somewhere down deep in his mind he was sure that yesterday at lunch, when he had been thinking about a magical place that only kids could visit, someone must have been listening. Before him he saw a huge, open city square paved with enormous marble slabs sprinkled with silver dust! It reminded Johnny of the sea, how it had looked the day before at the amusement park. But these were no ordinary paving stones, when you stepped on them they let out a sweet melody that spread out over the square like a gentle breeze.

"Mystery marble," his sister, Maria, would have called it if she'd been there, Johnny impressively thought, as he took a few steps forward.

Thousands of little streets and alleyways started from the square and disappeared behind the most beautiful, colorful houses Johnny had ever seen. There was so much traffic that Johnny stopped for a minute, trying to understand what was going on. Cars of every imaginable variety, together with all kinds of other contraptions, were racing around the square. And the air was filled with all kinds of flying things like, magic carpets, airplanes, flying pumpkins, birds, even dragons!!! Along with all the traffic in the square, there were thousands of creatures, small and large, familiar and strange, coming and going before Johnny's eyes. Look! There was the Little Magician, flying over his head on his magic carpet, off on an errand. Johnny could have spent hours gazing on this magical scene, if Chubby hadn't pulled him gently by the hand. "Come on, you'll have all the time you need to see everything and meet everyone!"

Johnny could not help but notice something very important. Wherever you looked, you saw children in the crowd. Some were busy doing something, while others were just sitting and talking to their magical friends; some were eating and drinking, while others were dancing and singing and playing different games. But all of them seemed very happy. Oh, how wonderful everything was here! As impossible as it seemed, Johnny felt so comfortable here that it was as if he had been here before, as if it were a place he knew and loved. Thinking these thoughts, Johnny followed on Chubby's heels, moving forward through the crowd, looking right and left at all the familiar faces from the cartoons and fairytales he had seen and read. There was the Cat in Blue Boots walking with the Girl in a red hat, and over there a pig with a wolf stood in front of a little well, talking and laughing. Gosh! What an incredible place this was. And the most incredible thing was that he was there, too!

"Come on," Chubby said to him, "Fire-bubble Rocketman is going to show you around. You'll get to see everything, and really fast, too!"

That, was what Johnny was most afraid of he had found himself here so suddenly that he was afraid everything might just as suddenly disappear. But his new friend, as if he could read Johnny's mind, reassured him, saying, "You're a regular member of our magical world now, Johnny. Don't worry, you can come whenever you want, we'll be here for you whenever you need us. Look, there's Fire-bubble Rocketman. It's his job to show the new kids around. Firebubble Rocket-man shows all the kids around Dreamland when they come for the first time, so they can get to know it really well, and fast..." The end of Chubby's sentence dis-solved into giggles.

"Hi, Johnny," Firebubble Rocketman said. Yet again, Johnny found himself not believing his own eyes or ears. It really was Firebubble Rocketman standing before him, talking to him.

"Um, hi," he choked out.

"Are you ready for a ride?"

"Of course, Firebubble Rocketman! I can't believe you're even asking!" Johnny said, trying to hide his enthusiasm. "I'm ready, let's go!"

Before he knew it, he was in Firebubble Rocketman's arms, flying over the colorful buildings and weaving between whatever or whoever else happened to be flying around in the air, too. For a moment he lost his breath and he was a little scared. But in a few seconds his fear had vanished and he had started to laugh because the wind was tickling his body all over.

"Look, down there," Firebubble Rocketman said, pointing out a beautiful cluster of tiny blue houses. The grass was bright green and the roofs of the houses were red with white polka dots. "That's where the Tiny People live. And over that way is where Golden Princess, Princess Azia, Girl with the beautifull hair, and all the other beautiful girls from fairytales from all over the world live." Looking down from between Firebubble Rocketman's arms, Johnny saw a number of huge castles, one right next to the other. They all had beautiful, fantastic gardens, and he could see Golden Princess watering the flowers in one of them. She saw them from afar and waved up at them, a wide smile on her face. Johnny waved back, but he wasn't sure if Golden Princess saw him because Firebubble Rocketman was moving from castle to castle so fast. "Look, this is where the Man with the Brave heart, the Great Wizard, and all of their friends live!" Firebubble Rocketman continued. "And down there is where all the Super Heroes live. And do you see that stable nestled down there in that field? That's where Blacky lives."

He and Firebubble Rocketman flew from neighborhood to neighborhood all day long. Or was it all night? Johnny had lost his sense of time. Either way, Dreamland just seemed to go on and on, there was no way you could see it all in a single trip, and so eventually the time came when they had to go back. Johnny didn't want to go back, everything he saw was so exciting that he wished the tour would never end.

They found Chubby waiting for them in the square with the "mystery marble." "How was it?" he asked when Johnny and Firebubble Rocketman landed on the ground next to him.

"You'll have to ask our friend here," Firebubble Rocketman said, laughing, "I think he enjoyed himself, and at least got a taste of Dreamland."

What could Johnny say then? He took a deep breath, opened his mouth, and a flood of words came pouring out. "Oh, Chubby, it was so wonderful, I saw so many things, Dreamland is unbelievable, I want to see more and more and more."

"Well," Chubby cut in, "you'll see it all, bit by bit. You'll meet everyone, too, and we'll have such a good time from now on! But for now, Firebubble Rocketman should be going on his way, there are other children waiting for him."

"Thanks so much, Firebubble Rocketman," Johnny said. "It was an incredible ride, and I hope we can do it again sometime."

"Sure thing!" Firebubble Rocketman answered. Then he waved goodbye and was gone in a flash.

What an amazing time! Who would believe him if Johnny told them tomorrow all he had seen and done? But right now that didn't matter.

Right now all that mattered was the fact that magic things really do happen in life, and Johnny was in Dreamland and felt so happy that he couldn't even begin to express his happiness to Chubby and all the others.

Walking toward the gate from the big square, they found themselves in front of a cart where a snowman was selling ice cream. All around the cart were little blue tables with tiny green chairs. They got some ice cream and sat down at one of the tables to rest for a while and enjoy their ice cream.

"You know, it's getting late, and soon you'll have to go back. But you should know that we're always here, and every time you go to sleep you can come to see us. We'll always be waiting for you so we can play, and if you ever need us in some time of trouble, we'll be here to help. Here in Dreamland, we teach children that the world is full of magic, and that it's a very beautiful and colorful place. We teach them to be strong and smart, to be good friends, and lots of other useful and important things that will help them get through the difficult times they're facing, and will also help them at other times in their lives."

When he'd heard all that, it occurred to Johnny that maybe he hadn't ended up in Dreamland entirely by chance. The time was definitely right, because his new friends could surely help him get over his illness. Because the truth was that on his own he didn't really know what to do, and he had been very upset at suddenly finding himself in the hospital.

"Thanks so much, Chubby!" Johnny answered, once he'd come back out of his thoughts. "Dreamland was fantastic! I can't wait to come again tomorrow and see more things. But how will I find my way back?" he asked, suddenly worried.

"Look, here are Daisy and Loli to take you to the gate, and tomorrow I'll be waiting there in the same spot so we can talk again. See you then," Chubby said. Daisy took Johnny's right hand, Loli took his left hand, and laughing and telling him stories they walked him as far as the gate, where they said goodbye and gave him a bright blue daisy with green polka dots to take with him.

19

Johnny hadn't even had time to wave goodbye when... he opened his eyes and what did he see? The sun shining outside the window of his hospital room! It was just past eight o'clock and his mother's face, smiling but tired, full of secret anxiety, was bending over him. "How are you feeling today?"

Johnny, despite all the adventures he'd had during the previous night, was bursting with joy and felt much better and more hopeful than he had the day before.

"Good morning, Mom! You won't believe what I did last night in my sleep, and where my dreams took me!" And he started to describe it all to his mother, down to the smallest detail.

"That's wonderful, darling. That sounds like a lovely dream. But come here and get washed up, the doctors are going to be here soon to see you and give you your medicine," his mother said after she'd listened carefully to Johnny's excited account of his adventures in Dreamland. Her words brought him back to reality, and Johnny suddenly fell silent. He really didn't feel like seeing the doctors again. He got up to wash, but it wasn't easy. There were lots of tubes hooked up to his body to give him medicines and fluids, and the tubes made each little movement very difficult. "I wish I were free," Johnny thought, looking up at the big metal contraption with its bottles and tubes. "I wish!"

Then he suddenly remembered the colorful daisy the two girls had given him as he was leaving Dreamland the night before, and wondered if it all had been true. "Where could it be?" he asked himself.

He looked around the room, but he didn't see anything. Then something made him pick up his pillow. And there they were, the blue petals of the flower, lying against the bright white hospital sheet. "Mom, Mom!" Johnny shouted, but before his mom could get there, the flower made an almost inaudible sound, a little "Puff," and vanished. "It's nothing, never mind," Johnny said to his mom. Suddenly Dreamland seemed very far away.

Those beautiful memories and images from the previous night started to lose their color. Before all the difficult things he was facing that day, his joy vanished just like the flower, and worry filled his little heart.

"It was all just a dream. How can Chubby and my new friends help me?

I bet they can't." And Johnny was overcome with hopelessness. He turned toward the wall and lay there all day with the blanket pulled up to his chin, not talking to anyone. The doctors came. They examined him and then left. The news didn't seem to be very good. Something wasn't going as well as everyone had expected, and he had to take some more medicine. All day long his mother kept trying to cheer him up, but there wasn't much she could do, so in the end she just sat there stroking his head until he fell asleep.

As soon as Johnny showed up in Dreamland that night, everyone could tell that something was wrong.

"What's wrong?" Hannah asked. Hannah was a very polite little girl from a fairytale from a distant country called Holland.

"I'm a little upset," Johnny said, "but mostly because I'm so tired! I don't want to go back to the hospital. They keep making me take all kinds of awful medicine and I have to do whatever the doctors say! And I can't, I don't like the pills. Besides, I don't think I'm ever going to get better!" (Of course, everyone in Dreamland knew perfectly well what Johnny was going through, just as they knew about every child who came to visit them.)

"I think that's all nonsense, little boy!" Hannah said severely. She was older than him, about twelve, so it was okay that she had called him little. "Come with me," she said, grabbing his hand and pulling him into a bakery at the edge of Silver Square. The bakery was called 1002 Little Candies, and they each ordered a bowl of strawberry-flavored sugared snowflakes. Then they sat down at a little table to eat and talk.

"Johnny," Hannah said, "I'm going to tell you about something that happened far away in my country, Holland. But before I tell you, I want you to try some of your sugared snowflakes and tell me if you like them."

Johnny tried them and they tasted wonderful, like something straight out of a dream. "Of course, I like them!" he answered.

Then Hannah turned to him and said, "Do you know why? Because you're supposed to like them, that's what they're for. They're a treat that we eat when we want something sweet and delicious, something that will make us happy. Right?"

"Right," Johnny answered doubtfully. He didn't really understand what Hannah was getting at.

"Well, Johnny, medicine isn't suppose to make us happy, it's suppose to help us get better. I'll teach you a trick. Just hold your nose and wash your medicine down with lots of water! You won't even taste it at all, I promise. And when you want a treat, something really tasty, that's when you eat sugared snowflakes. Okay?"

Johnny's mouth was full of snowflakes, so nodded his head to show her he agreed. He had understood completely, and deep down he knew that Hannah was right. So when he had swallowed and emptied his mouth and could talk again, he said to Hannah, "I get it now! I just hadn't thought about it that way. From now on I promise to take all my medicine without complaining a single bit, since I know it's for my own good!"

"That's great, Johnny! And now for that story I was going to tell you," Hannah said, and started to tell him her story.

"One day, my mother and I went for a walk in the forest to pick blackberries. Of course my mom had told me not to stray too far, and of course I didn't listen and wandered off. And so, of course, I got lost. The further I went into the forest, trying to find my way back to my mother, the more lost I got. Wherever I turned, the forest looked exactly the same and as it got later, the forest seemed to get denser and darker, too. Soon I'd gone so far that no one could hear me, no matter how much I shouted. I was very tired. I was hungry and thirsty and my feet were starting to hurt from so much walking. The trees were so dense and huge that when I looked up I could hardly see the sky. It had started to get really dark and I'd begun to lose all hope of ever finding my way home or seeing my mother again. Besides, I was starting to get afraid of the wolves that were coming out as night fell. Every so often I could hear them howling. So I sat down on a fallen tree trunk and started to cry.

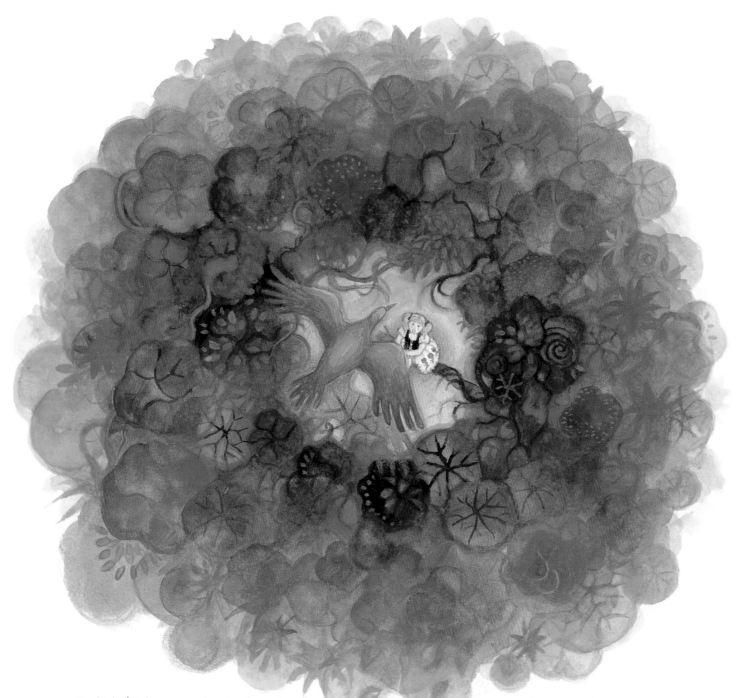

I didn't know what else to do. Suddenly, something made me wipe my eyes and raise them up to look at the sky.

And in that tiny little sliver of sky, painted with the last light of day, way up there between the enormous branches of the trees, I saw a huge blue bird. It was flying in circles exactly over my head, as if silently inviting me to follow it.

So that's what I did, I watched it flying overhead, and followed where it led. And the big blue bird led me out of the forest, right into the arms of my mother, who had been searching for me for hours. Her joy at that moment was more than words can describe. First we cried, then we laughed, then she scolded me-and rightly so-and then I promised her I would never do it again. On the way home, I asked her about the big blue bird that had helped me find my way out of the forest. She told me its name was 'Hope,' and that it lives eternally and never dies and always follows people in their difficult moments and helps them persevere. That's how I learned that I should never lose hope. I told you that story because I thought you might find it helpful, too."

By now they had finished their strawberry-flavored sugared snowflakes. Johnny thanked Hannah for keeping him company and for telling him her wonderful story, which had taught him lots of things. His mood had improved considerably, and after he said good-bye to Hannah, who was in a hurry because she and Daisy were going shopping for shoes and she didn't want to be late, Johnny ran to find Chubby to take him as far as the gate. It was late and he needed to be getting back.

When he woke up the next morning, Johnny was a model patient. He took all his medicine without complaining, listened carefully to what the doctors told him and followed their orders without a second thought.

"What happened, Johnny?" his mother asked, baffled. "Yesterday we had to beg you a thousand times to take a single pill."

Johnny told her, very soberly, that he had done a lot of serious thinking the night before and had realized that the medicine was for his own good. Then he told her he hoped he would get better soon.

"Of course you will, Johnny, darling!" his mom cried, together with his dad, who had just walked into the room and had heard everything Johnny had been saying "For us, it's not just a matter of hope, we're convinced you'll get better very, very soon!"

They hugged him very tightly, and sitting there snug in their arms Johnny understood that everything would be just fine, because now he knew how badly he wanted to get better. And so he fell asleep again.

"Guys, guys!" Johnny cried. By now, Dreamland had become like a second home to him. Right then he was surrounded by Flyheart the warrior, Silver Shadow, and Pink Rabbit, who was munching on a carrot. "Yesterday, I was talking to my mom and I told her I had learned what it means to want something with all your heart. And, right now, what I want with all my heart is to get well. But I'm not sure I can do it on my own. Can you guys help me?"

"Of course!", everyone agreed right away to help him. "Hmm, what should you do? What should you do?" Pink Rabbit said, thinking out loud. They were all in thought, trying to find that special something that would help Johnny strengthen his will and determination.

For a moment there was absolute silence. "Hey, I've got it!" Flyheart the warrior, shouted, full of enthusiasm. "Today, Johnny, you're going to fly!"

By the way, Flyheart was a warrior from the Kingdom of Up-Up and Beyond. He was wearing his light blue, silvery armour and his pointy wings fluttered lightly around him. He carried his sword always with him and seemed very confident and prepared.

"But how?" Johnny asked doubtfully. It sounded like a great idea, but he didn't know how he could do it.

"Yep, that's it. The old familiar recipe. All you need is faith and trust, and a little bit of pixie dust! Are you ready?" Flyheart, excited by his idea. The rest of the group agreed that it was a very good way for Johnny to test his strength.

"So?" Flyheart, asked again. "Are you ready to try?"

"I don't know," Johnny answered. Then he added, thoughtful but determined, "I guess we'll see!" He closed his eyes and concentrated on wanting to fly with all the strength in his soul. He sat like that for a while, until he felt something tickling him on the face.

He opened his left eye a crack and saw something sparkling before him. Pixie dust! But he knew that wasn't enough to make him fly.

So he closed his eyes again very, very tightly, imagined an enormous, shining rainbow, and wanted with all his heart to fly-and suddenly he felt his feet slowly lifting from the ground! It was as if he didn't weigh anything, he felt like a feather in the air. In the air!!! Then suddenly he became aware of someone shouting into his ear. It was Fly-heart, who was crying with all his heart. "See? You did it! You did it!"

Johnny gathered up all his courage and slowly opened his eyes. Wow! It was true! He was flying! He was flying! Flyheart was flying in circles around him and shouting to make himself heard over the breeze. "See, nothing is impossible. It's up to you to make it happen! What do you say, should I teach you a few tricks?"

"Yes, yes, I really want to learn!" Johnny shouted between his laughter-the breeze was tickling him all over his body.

"Spread your arms like you're an airplane," Flyheart began, "and then dive up or down. If you want to stop, just raise your head a little. If you want to turn, lean your body to the left or right, and if you want to stay still, cross your hands on your chest. It's that simple. You can stay there in place as long as you want. I'll teach you how to do somersaults later. Let's practice for a while first and see how it goes. So, what do you say, are you ready?"

Johnny didn't answer, because he was concentrating on mentally repeating all the moves he had just been shown. As soon as he was sure he could remember each and every one, he spread his arms and soared up into the clouds, cutting through the air like an arrow, trying to catch up with Flyheart. After a few ungainly turns, he could do the moves as if he'd been flying all his life.

In his head he tried to find words to describe the amazing feeling of flying. It reminded him a little of being with his parents in the car when there was a big hill in front of them and

then a big dip down. On the downward slope, he and Maria would yell for their dad to drive as fast as he could. They would raise their arms over their heads and their tummies would turn into little balls inching up their throats, and they would burst into gales of laughter. Or else it was like swinging so hard on a swing that you think you can touch the sky with your feet, and it feels like something is tickling you from your feet to the top of your head. All of that and more was what Johnny was feeling right then, soaring through the clouds. But stronger than anything was the feeling that he could do anything. Whatever he wanted, as long as he wanted it very, very badly.

After Flyheart had shown Johnny his last tricks, they decided to go back, because it was getting late. And so, taking one last spin in the air, they headed towards the place where Silver shadow, and Pink Rabbit, Chubby, and lots of others were waiting for them. The news about Johnny's success had spread quickly, so everyone was waiting impatiently for him to come back and tell them about his new experience.

And they sure didn't have to twist Johnny's arm. As soon as his feet touched ground he started to tell everyone how wonderful it was to fly. "I wish all children could fly!" he said again and again, trying to pull himself together. "I don't think there's anything better in the whole wide world!"

"Don't worry, you're not the only one. Everyone flies in their sleep at one time or another! And of course they say that when you fly in your sleep it means you're growing up!" Chubby said. "Come on, though, I'll take you to the gate, because it's very late and you need to be getting back."

Johnny, after he had hugged Flyheart tightly and thanked him for everything, said goodbye to the whole crowd and followed Chubby, murmuring, "Even time is magical here in Dreamland, it passes without you even realizing!"

"I hope today taught you a lot," Chubby said, smiling.

Johnny, smiled back, waved goodbye and passed through the gate... and opened his eyes to see the first rays of the sun coming in through the curtains of his hospital room.

"Good morning," his mother said. She had been sleeping in the bed next to him each night during his stay at the hospital. "How did you sleep?"

"Great, Mom, I've never slept better," Johnny replied, stretching his little body. Was he stiff from sleeping or from flying? Who knew?

He had a difficult week in front of him, but now he knew what he wanted very, very badly, to get well. So he was a model patient, following his doctor's orders faithfully, down to the letter. And most importantly, he stayed in good spirits the whole time. Except for Sunday, when something happened. Something that shook Johnny's faith a lot.

It was Sunday morning and after another night of adventures in Dreamland, where he and his friends had arranged all the details for a soccer match to take place the following day, Johnny had woken up full of hope and optimism. He was sitting with his parents in his room, waiting for the doctors to come, because today they would be bringing very important news about the development of Johnny's health.

The time was passing a little more slowly today, but together they talked and played until at last time came for the doctors' visit. As always, they came into the room, examined him, told a few jokes, asked if he hurt anywhere, and then went back out into the hall with his parents.

The news wasn't good. Johnny should have been getting better, but for some reason his health still wasn't improving. It was a mystery to the doctors, who still hadn't managed to figure it out.

When he heard the news, Johnny grew very sad. He was so disappointed that in just a few minutes his faith and confidence were completely shattered. He felt like he would never get better. His parents kept trying to convince him that it didn't mean anything and that sooner or later things would start to improve, but Johnny didn't listen to any of it and fell asleep, sunk in the dark thoughts that had overwhelmed him.

"Come on, Johnny, we've been waiting for you," Chubby said. "Today's the big day! This game is going to be so much fun!"

Everything had been arranged. On Johnny's team were Chubby, the Little Magician, Pinoccello, the Green Giant and two other children, Joe and Pano, who had started visiting Dreamland recently. On the other team, with the Elf, were also three children, Alex, Demitri and Charlie. Anyhow, the game had been arranged for a while, so everyone was waiting for him impatiently, and a big crowd of spectators had gathered to watch. Arriving at the field, Johnny briefly forgot the black thoughts that had taken hold of his mind. Looking out at the field, he smiled. The grass was green, of course, but sometimes when it got bored of being the same color for too long, it would change from green to orange, then yellow, then some other color. Right at that moment it was red. The members of the two teams put on their uniforms and waited for the last stragglers to arrive.

Suddenly, while they were all sitting there and Johnny was talking to Chubby, the sky started to grow dark. Johnny looked up at the sky and what did he see? Black clouds appearing out of nowhere, just like everything else in this magical place. Within a few seconds the entire sky had gone black and it had started to rain! Oh no! What a disappointment!!!

"No game now. What should we do?" Johnny's disappointment and despair were so great that tears started to flow down his cheeks without him even realizing it. He had been looking forward to this game so much....

Suddenly he remembered that one day, not long before, he and the Good Fairy had been sitting in the square and talking. There was a question that had been plaguing Johnny for a long time, and he figured the time had come for him to ask it.

"Good Fairy, can you tell me why I'm always healthy when I come here to Dreamland but when I go back in the morning I'm still so sick?"

"Listen, Johnny, it does not matter where you are or what you do.

What matters is what you really want. Magic can happen everywhere because it's inside us. It's in our hearts. Remember that. Always remember that!" the Good Fairy had said.

Now, looking up at the black sky, Johnny remembered that conversation. So he squeezed his eyes shut and wished with all the strength in his soul for the sun to come out again. He stayed like that for a while, believing very, very strongly.

Then he slowly opened his eyes, and what did he see? He had done his first magic thing! The sky wasn't black anymore-the rain had stopped, the clouds had disappeared and the most beautiful, glowing rainbow he'd ever seen in his life had come out. Pano and Charlie ran up and hugged him. Chubby and all the rest of his friends were all standing right next to him, smiling smiles full of meaning. Yes! It was the rainbow of hope and faith.

 "See what you did?" they all shouted at once. "Each of us has a magic power inside, you just proved it to everybody, but most important to yourself....

"I see now!" Johnny said, his face lighting up with a smile full of self-confidence.

The game took place, they had a wonderful time and the next morning when Johnny found himself in his hospital room he started to think about everything that had happened in Dreamland. His mother was right beside him as always, and that day she noticed a certain light in Johnny's eyes. It was a little flickering flame that had always been there, but that had recently disappeared. She was very happy to see it again. Of course she had no way of knowing about everything Johnny had been through in Dreamland, and there was no way for Johnny to explain. There are some things that adults don't understand, things that are only for children. But he had a plan of his own to show her all he had learned there. To make magic, that is.

That day Johnny started to get better, hour by hour. And with each passing day, when the doctors came to see him, they couldn't believe their eyes.

Every night, leaving for his magic journey to Dreamland, he whispered to his mother, "I love sleeping! I love to sleep!" And he would close his eyes with a smile, because he knew the next morning when he would wake up he would be stronger, more able to achieve what he wanted so badly, as hard as it might be. And Johnny did his second magic thing, he conquered his illness!!!

The day came for Johnny to leave the hospital and go home. Everyone there had been waiting for him so long, particularly his sister Maria. Johnny knew that he would be able to describe to her all his adventures in Dreamland, and that she would under-stand, since she was a child, too. He might even be able to take her along one night to introduce her to all his friends. And he could tell her all that he had learned about friendship, hope, and faith. All those things would be very useful to her in her whole life, too–and perhaps he could even teach her to do magic!

Everything went well. Johnny went back to school. One by one the years passed, he went off to college, he worked hard, he grew big and strong.... but each night when he went to sleep, he still tried to go to Dreamland. He wanted to see his old friends there, to learn their news, to relive all those moments that had filled his heart with such love and kindness.

... But no matter how hard he tried, only children can visit Dreamland and by now Johnny was Mr. John. He had grown up. Still, every night when he went to sleep he would say to himself. "I love to sleep! I love sleeping!" And he would fall sleep with a wide, happy smile on his face, because he knew that if you want something strongly enough and believe in it with all your heart, you can always make it happen... even a miracle!!

MARIA ZACHARIA

She was born and spent her childhood years in Moscow, Russia until her family moved to Athens, Greece in 1980. There she married and had two children. When her son became sick with leukemia, the family moved to Memphis, Tennessee, so her son could be treated at St. Jude Children's Research Hospital. "Little Johnny's Dreamland" is her first book.

Little Johnny's Dreamland
P.O. Box 3341 • Memphis, TN 38173-0341

To order, please provide the following information:

Name: _____

Street Address: _____

City:_____ State: _____ Zip:_____

Daytime Phone:_____ Email Address: _____

	Quantity	Price each	Total Amount
Little Johnny's Dreamland		$19.95	_____
Tennessee residents add 9.75% sales tax			_____
If books are to be mailed add $5.00 each shipping & handling			_____
Total amount			_____

Send Check or Money Order to:

Little Johnny's Dreamland
P.O. Box 3341 • Memphis, TN 38173-0341

Little Johnny's Dreamland
P.O. Box 3341 • Memphis, TN 38173-0341

To order, please provide the following information:

Name: _____

Street Address: _____

City:_____ State: _____ Zip:_____

Daytime Phone:_____ Email Address: _____

	Quantity	Price each	Total Amount
Little Johnny's Dreamland		$19.95	_____
Tennessee residents add 9.75% sales tax			_____
If books are to be mailed add $5.00 each shipping & handling			_____
Total amount			_____

Send Check or Money Order to:

Little Johnny's Dreamland
P.O. Box 3341 • Memphis, TN 38173-0341

Little Johnny's Dreamland
P.O. Box 3341 • Memphis, TN 38173-0341

To order, please provide the following information:

Name: _____

Street Address: _____

City:_____ State: _____ Zip:_____

Daytime Phone:_____ Email Address: _____

	Quantity	Price each	Total Amount
Little Johnny's Dreamland		$19.95	_____
Tennessee residents add 9.75% sales tax			_____
If books are to be mailed add $5.00 each shipping & handling			_____
Total amount			_____

Send Check or Money Order to:

Little Johnny's Dreamland
P.O. Box 3341 • Memphis, TN 38173-0341

Little Johnny's Dreamland
P.O. Box 3341 • Memphis, TN 38173-0341

To order, please provide the following information:

Name: _____

Street Address: _____

City:_____ State: _____ Zip:_____

Daytime Phone:_____ Email Address: _____

	Quantity	Price each	Total Amount
Little Johnny's Dreamland		$19.95	_____
Tennessee residents add 9.75% sales tax			_____
If books are to be mailed add $5.00 each shipping & handling			_____
Total amount			_____

Send Check or Money Order to:

Little Johnny's Dreamland
P.O. Box 3341 • Memphis, TN 38173-0341